MW00622348

ISBN (print): 978-1-7773486-7-0

ISBN (ebook): 978-1-7773486-8-7

Cover design and graphics by Marcus Hawke

PRAISE FOR THE MIRACLE SIN

"A rollercoaster of horror and tension."

MICHAEL BENAVIDEZ, AUTHOR
OF *WHEN ANGELS FAIL: AS THE
SHADOWS GROW*

"This book does not hold back, it does not shy away from the nitty-gritty, and certainly keeps you coming back for more."

SABRINA VOERMAN, AUTHOR
OF *ÆSA*

"A tragic, grueling journey of self-reflection, with beloved characters who now hold a special place in my heart. Mason is a relatable MC, and I felt like a part of the story as I joined him in his endeavors. Marcus is one incredible writer. His attention to detail is something to be admired, and I thoroughly enjoyed the flow, structure, and pace of *The Miracle Sin*. Profound themes, charming characters, and a lot of great laughs await you! One of my favorite reads of 2021."

SHANNON LANE, AUTHOR OF
TEMPERANCE

"I can't say enough for this masterwork. It's clever and funny as hell while being torturously terrifying."

"Marcus does great work in this book, he has an eye for character and writes with wit and elegant style. He can brutal yet tender at once. I can't wait to read what he does next."

"This is exactly the kind of story that I live for; something deep enough to get lost in, a world created and unveiled for me to explore, to find wonder and horror alike. A story that makes me think, makes me ask questions and makes me wonder at what else this world may hold."

"As I sit here trying to write this review, I am finding myself to be at a loss for words. That is something that rarely happens...I found this to be absolutely wonderful in every way possible. The prose is stunning, the characters are well developed, and the themes are a medley, filled with some brutal moments, and yet there is a tenderness that is heartfelt. Religious undertones that makes the mind question, loss of human life, human suffering and questioning faith...I just love the depth of this and it has nestled itself into my soul."

KARLA PETERSON, AMAZON
REVIEW

"Admittedly I'm not the biggest thriller/horror fan so I went into this a little unsure. However, Marcus reminded me that it's not just the story but how you tell it and he did a phenomenal job telling Mason's! Several times I caught myself rereading a line because I was so impressed with how well written it was."

BEE DAVIS, AMAZON REVIEW

"The book has quite the action in it with just the right amount of blood and guts. There we're definitely a few scenes that had me clutching my pearls and going for my smelling salts."

GRACE REYNOLDS, AUTHOR OF
LADY OF THE HOUSE

"I need a sequel. Stat!"

REBECCA ROSSI, AUTHOR OF
THE DEVIL IN ME

PRAISE FOR ACTS OF VIOLENCE

"Horrible in the best way!"

HEATHER MIHOK, AUTHOR OF
THE INN-SITTER

"A well-written collection that makes you shake your head and then smile seconds after."

E.C. HANSON, AUTHOR OF
WICKED BLOOD

"It's always a rarity when I can sing praise for every single story in a collection. Well, Sir Hawke has done it people, he's created a pearl here, through several years of pressure and build up--one with loads of mentally tortured characters and brutalized bodies."

ALANA K. DREX, AUTHOR OF
SLEEPING CELESTE

"I'm not one for short story collections, but I couldn't pass up the opportunity to read more of his work and this did not disappoint. You'll be hard pressed to find a collection that gives you the willies like this one does."

CALEB RYAN,
@THE_BOOKEYMAN

"Marcus's writing feels so effortless as it carries you from story to story. I tend to be a rather critical reader despite my best efforts so collections are typically a mixed bag for me. Acts of violence is one of the only collections I've read that every single story was good, compelling, interesting... all in different ways but all thoroughly enjoyable."

GWENDOLYN WOOD,
@GWENREADSHORROR

"This was a quick read and honestly, it was hard for me to put down...I absolutely love short story collections and this is one I'm definitely going to be re reading later on."

DAISY RODRIGUEZ,
@CHIBICHAPTERS

"Dark humor mixed with engaging descriptive text along with unique takes on well used tropes, makes these stories captivating, disturbing and completely enjoyable."

"This is a gruesome buffet of the uncanny, the weird, the gory, the supernatural, the strange and disgusting, with a glorious dark humour seasoning, delicious!"

BE ADVISED

This book will not make you feel better.

It won't be your comfort read nor your escape from the dumpster fire of reality. It contains sad facts, uncomfortable truths, and hard pills to swallow. And while there's no dog in this story, if there were it wouldn't be ok.

It's that kind of story.

It also deals with the topics of depression, suicide, intrusive and morbid thoughts, family dysfunction, and other mature subject matter.

"Television is reality.
And reality is less than television."

DAVID CRONENBERG'S
VIDEODROME

PLAY ▶

GREY NOISE

MARCUS HAWKE

RIGHT WHERE IT BELONGS

EVAN GREY SLAMMED on the brakes, bringing his van to a grinding halt. The screech of the tires echoed across Frobisher Street, an unremarkable stretch of road in a neighborhood that was the right kind of shady on what was sure to be a hot summer's day. The coffee he had just bought stayed secure in the cup holder next to him while the box of donuts in the passenger's seat jerked forward and onto the floor. His beady eyes, looking for nothing in particular except for where to turn, went wide as they fell upon the very thing he had been searching for these past several months, but he'd never expected to find here and now. Sitting right there on the curb was an old vacuum tube television set.

"No way!"

He reversed until the object in the mirror was as close as it appeared. A 29" Panasonic, just like he used to have years ago. It was clean, the screen was intact, and there was hardly a scratch to be found. It could have been left there moments ago, as if patiently waiting there for him. Taped to it was a full piece of plain white paper with the single greatest word a small business owner could hope to see written on it in big black felt letters.

FREE

All it was missing was a bow.

Evan got out and opened the back doors of the van.

His long brown hair momentarily hung in his face, full with the slight hang of a double chin, obscuring his view as he knelt down and picked it up off the ground. Heavy as hell compared to the televisions of today, but he managed to get it up into the hold of the van with little fuss. With the biggest smile you ever did see, Evan tucked his hair back behind his ears and returned to the driver's seat. It was just the right thing to make this the perfect day.

He checked the time on his phone—July 18, 9:50 AM—before pulling away from the curb and continuing on his way.

The sun was already beating down hard. With the window rolled down there came a nice breeze as he cruised the city streets, stale with the dry summer air and slightly sour with the smell of gas fumes. Cars rushed about, occasionally honking at each other. A muggy haze from the heat gave the buildings of downtown a sort of sweltering, mirage-like quality in the distance. A thick layer of smog clung to the air above like a stain on the sky. It was as nice a view a concrete jungle like this could afford. The Lovin' Spoonful's "Summer in the City" began playing on the radio, and as the lyrics suggested, Evan could already feel the back of his neck getting dirty and gritty.

As he passed a few buildings smeared with graffiti, there, at the tail end of a strip mall and across the lot from a gas station, was his pride and joy—REWIND VIDEO.

Right away there was the GRAND OPENING banner in the window just below the custom red and blue neon sign he had made. Good. That was the idea. Every bit of exposure and visibility he could get. He had spent the last nine months renovating, refurbishing, and in some cases rebuilding this spot. Every day, every morning, often until late at night. Dealing with contractors, safety inspectors, business licenses, building permits, distributors, manufacturers, private collectors, and fellow owners. But for the most part, doing the work himself with his own two hands. He could have found it with his eyes closed at this point. It was worth it.

This was his baby.

Okay, so he spent the last of his savings fixing it up, and even downgraded from his apartment to what, he was pretty sure, was supposed to be a break room above that came with the store. But so what? At thirty-four years old, and having worked in his stepdad's hardware store since he was seventeen, it was time to take a few chances. Past time, in fact. Ten years ago would have been better but hey, how about that hindsight, right? From lack of money, lack of inspiration, lack of options, and lack of explanations he had just plodded along, towing the line at Hank's Hardware. And in the end, it was lack of patience that led to his unceremonious departure.

Evan eased into the spot in front of the store and got the TV from the back of his van before heading to the door.

BEE-BOO, went the door as he propped it open with his elbow, hugging the TV in both arms. He set it down on the nearby counter at the other end from the register. The smell of popcorn hit him right away, and with it a wave of buttery endorphins. Taking care to angle it out toward the main area of the store, he made sure the screen was visible to anyone there. Once it was plugged in, he hit the ON button.

Kshhhhhhhhhhhhhhhhhhhhhhhhhhhhhhhhhhhhhhh . . .

Static.

To be expected. It wasn't wired for cable, and he didn't need it for that. But it worked, that's all that mattered.

"Too bad you didn't come with a remote," said Evan, pressing the UP button on the front of the TV to change the channel. When the number in the corner of the screen flipped from Channel 5 to Channel 6, he pressed the down button instead until it came finally to good ol' Channel 3.

Kshhhhhhhhhhhhhhhhhhhhhhhhhhhhhhhhhhhhhh . . .
Still.

"Hmm…" It had been a while since he hooked one of these up, but the basic premise was the same. Evan switched the input and the static turned to a field of solid azure with VIDEO in the top right corner.

"It's alive!" cried Evan. "Mwahaha! Now," he said, fluttering his fingers as he surveyed the wall of tapes behind the counter, "what shall we use to christen this baby?"

Predator? Too loud.

Flash Gordon? Too niche.

Porky's? Too bawdy.

Dirty Dancing? What are you, a girl?

Even now he could still hear Hank's voice in his head when he had found him watching that one day. He made him turn it off and watch *Patton* instead. Evan liked sports too—*Go Pats!*—he liked to BBQ, knew about cars and everything else a man was supposed to know. What he didn't do was tell people they're girls for watching a movie, or for having long hair, or poke fun at people who aren't in peak physical condition. The only movies Hank liked had either Clint Eastwood, Charlton Heston, or the Duke.

"Go ahead," Hank had said when Evan quit. He laughed and stood there with his hands on his hips and that shit-eating grin on his face. *"Go waste time and money with your stupid movies and games and Space Trek bullshit. You'll be back."*

5

Evan pushed the unwelcome voice from his mind. *Die Hard? Maybe if it were close to Christmas. Robocop? No, but closer. Ghostbusters? Closer. Jurassic Park. Closer. Something with the Spielberg touch.*

Then he spotted it. The perfect one—*Back to the Future.*

Evan relocated the VCR, tucked away down below, to the space behind the TV for easier access, slid the tape into the slot and pressed PLAY. The screen turned from blue to black. And then...

Kshhhhhhhhhhhhhhhhhhhhhhhhhhhhhhhhhhhhhh . . .

"What?"

shhhhhhhhhhhhhhhhhhhhhhhhhhhhhhhhhhhhhh . . .

"Why?"

Everything was done right. Power, check. Channel 3, check. Input, check.

"Oh, for god sake!"

The cables. He connected the RCA cables to the inputs at the back. Red to red, yellow to yellow, white to white.

Still nothing.

Somehow, he didn't think the all-powerful maxim of "Have you tried turning it off and on again?" would work on an analog device. So Evan did what anyone experiencing technical difficulties does—he hit it. A few good slaps on one side and finally the static was knocked out just in time, replaced with the synthesized opening notes of "The Power of Love". Music to his ears.

Evan pumped his fist triumphantly in the air like Judd Nelson and let it blast through the hold of the ship he had built.

It still amazed him sometimes. A faithfully, painstakingly recreated video store. Straight out of the '80s and '90s. And to that end, no title in the store went past the date of 1999. It had been a porn store before. Now, it was an experience. Cardboard VHS boxes on wire racks placed through the storeroom floor to make a simple grid of aisles, proudly bearing titles like *The Goonies, Beverly Hills Cop, Caddyshack, The Karate Kid,* and *The Land Before Time.* The actual tapes were kept behind the counter in plastic cases on shelves labelled in alphabetical order, as they should be.

Evan had placed every collectible and piece of memorabilia he had all around the store. T-800s, and starship Enterprises, and more than one lightsaber beaming brightly colored light along the walls. Signed headshots from the likes of Sylvester Stallone and Sigourney Weaver. An Alf and Bart Simpson doll perched on either side of the register. Some of it for sale, some not. It belonged here, that's what mattered. And the truth was that while he'd spent a lifetime collecting these things, he had nowhere else to keep it all.

Evan spent a lot of time and care and money curating things like a gumball machine. A *Street Fighter II* arcade game. A dollar bin for used movies, but of course these were all used. So he filled it with movies you might find in the dollar bin back in the day—*Captain Ron, Toys, Deuce Bigalow: Male Gigolo, Son in Law, Encino Man,* basically anything with Pauly Shore. A popcorn machine, complete with paper bags free to fill for customers. An Adult Section in what used to be a supply closet behind an opaque black shower curtain. The works. And above the door as people left, the almighty single commandment of the video store—BE KIND, PLEASE REWIND. In this case it not only encouraged people how to treat their tapes, but also to come again. All that had been missing was a TV—a proper, era-appropriate TV—to play movies on. Until today. It was just the stroke of luck he needed.

Evan took a step back and admired it all. Everything he had recreated, plucked out of his own memory. Resurrected. This had been his dream for as long as he could remember. Since he was a boy of nine, maybe ten years old. He had fond memories of movie nights with his dad that had begun at a place just like this. He taught him that if you put your mind to it you can accomplish anything. And he had learned that from George McFly.

His dad died when Evan was twelve. A penniless alcoholic musician. "By his own hand." Those were the words his mom chose when she told him. Words he was sure she chose to soften the blow.

It didn't.

And Hank was his replacement.

If people were still buying vinyl albums, why not

this? Perhaps it was fate that shortly after the seed of this venture had fully taken root that he'd had enough of this old job. He gave his notice, walked out the door, and never looked back. All the while hearing Hank's choice words for him.

Go ahead. You'll be back.

This store was more than just *his* baby; it belonged to his dad too. He knew he would be proud of him. And it was finally done. Things were looking up.

———

It was nearly time to open and everything was good to go, so Evan started stocking the Action Section.

Well, almost everything.

Brian still hadn't shown up. They had worked together at Dairy Queen in their sophomore year, just before Evan swallowed his pride in need of a steady paycheck working at Hank's. So Evan knew that this was nothing out of the ordinary. But still, best friends are supposed to be able to count on each other, right?

Ten o' clock came and went.

As did eleven.

And twelve.

Still no Brian. And still no customers.

Back to the Future was long over and had been replaced with *Ferris Bueller's Day Off*. By this point he had already eaten half the donuts he bought.

No big deal. I didn't expect people would come

rushing in or anything. But someone, anyone, would be nice. A single soul looking to revisit and reconnect with a little piece of a bygone era? A collector looking for the director's cut of *Blade Runner*? Maybe someone looking to replace a long lost tape of *E.T.* they had when they were a kid?

BEE-BOO went the door.

A woman with glasses poked her head in the door as Evan froze midway in taking another donut like a kid with his hand caught in the cookie jar.

"Hi, sorry, but can I just use your bathroom?" she spoke through gritted teeth as if to silently convey that she really hoped he would say yes, lest she piss right there at the front entrance of his store.

"Sure, no problem," Evan said, pointing toward the back.

She did her business and left, without saying thank you.

"You're welcome."

Not ten seconds later the door went again.

BEE-BOO

In walked a small elderly man wearing a cap and leisure wear. His face was wrinkled and spotty with eyes that seemed to be searching for something, but he didn't know what.

"Good day, sir. What can I do for you?"

He looked around, confused. "This ain't the porno shop."

"Oh…no, I'm afraid it closed."

"Closed?"

"Yes, sir."

A long moment passed in which Evan wasn't sure what else he was supposed to say or do.

"I just been away visiting my daughter in Tampa for a week, and it's closed?"

"I'm afraid so. Sorry."

The old man stared absently like he had just been told the Sox had won the World Series and he'd slept through it.

No way he's only been away for a week. "But we do have a selection of adult titles just behind that curtain there, if you're interested."

The old man turned, not his head, his whole body, to see where Evan was pointing, and then back to face him again. "Through there?"

"That's right."

And with a half-hearted wave, off he went behind the secretive backroom curtain.

Okay. Not what I had in mind, but a customer is a customer. He was actually really surprised anyone still did that when they could look it up on the internet with a few keystrokes. But then, the same could be said for any movie at all these days.

BEE-BOO

Evan turned around to see Brian, at long last, who came stumbling through the door. Hood pulled up, sunglasses, a beard long enough to braid, wearing board shorts and flip flops, and absolutely reeking of reefer.

11

"Yo, yo, yo," he warbled.

Evan looked at his watch. It was half past noon.

"Three hours late, Bry? Really?"

"Sorry, man But I had a crazy night."

"Yeah well, you can tell me all about it later," Evan interrupted, knowing full well if he started the tale he wouldn't stop. "There's a shirt for you in the office," he said, thumbing behind him.

"A shirt?"

Evan pointed at his own, proudly bearing REWIND VIDEO stitched into the left breast pocket in 8-bit lettering.

"Whoa, official and everything, hey? Right on, I'll be back in a jiff."

More like a spliff, Evan thought.

Brian headed toward the back and stopped at the counter. "Hey, when did you get the TV?"

"This morning," Evan said, the wide grin returning to his face. "Found it just sitting outside on Frobisher for zero bucks."

"Beauty, dude."

Brian disappeared through the door behind the counter and returned a short time later.

"Tada," he said, wearing his shirt backwards.

Evan gave him a look like he had just been told to live long and prosper on May the Fourth. "Very funny."

"Aw c'mon, I'm just trying to get a yuck outta ya."

"I know, I know. I just want today to go well, that's all."

"Isn't it?" Brian asked as he peeled the shirt off and put it on the right way.

"A little slow so far." His eyes shifted to the Adult Section where the Porn Man had gone. *Please God, don't let him be whacking off in there.* There were many things he had to put up with working at Hank's Hardware, but that was definitely not one of them.

"Meh, that's to be expected, first day and all right?"

"I guess."

"Besides," Brian made a gesture to entire store, "look at what you've done."

Evan was again almost moved to tears by the wave of nostalgia and the joy that came with it. "Yeah, you're right. Thanks man." Evan clapped Brian on the back. "Alright, assholes and elbows. Let's go."

"You ever get mistaken for a woman, Vasquez?"

"No. Have you?"

"Ha! Hey, when's lunch?"

"How about once you've been here longer than ten minutes?"

"You're the boss, Boss. Where do I start?"

"If you could finish stocking the Action Section, that would be awesome."

"No sweat, Boba Fett." And to the Action Section he went.

Evan poked his head through the other side of the naughty curtain. "How are we doing in here?"

What am I, working at the GAP?

"Well…" said the old man and trailed off.

Evan came the rest of the way in past the curtain to see that he was holding two titles in either hand, *The Sperminator* and *Four Wettings and a Few Anal.* Weighing them as if they were on a scale.

"I can't decide which to get," he said languidly.

BEE-BOO

Someone moved past the slit in the curtain.

"Okay well, just take your time then."

Definitely been away longer than a week.

With the back of his hand, Evan tucked back the edge of the curtain. Two young girls had entered. One had chin-length hair beneath a purple beanie, overalls, and a pair of round glasses perched high on her nose which was pierced at the septum, the other had an undercut swooped heavily to one side wearing a leather jacket and harem pants.

"Hello," he said emerging from behind the curtain once again. "Can I help you?"

"No," said purple beanie. "Just looking."

"Ok, well, let me know if you need anything."

Bloggers by the looks of them. Probably weren't even twenty years old yet and somehow managed to have 10K followers each on every social media platform imaginable by posting videos of them staring blankly while a five second audio clip and nondescript text did all the work.

"Bry," Evan stage whispered in the direction of the Action Section. Brian's head popped up like a gopher from a golf hole. Evan waved him over. "How do we land these two?" They went from shelf to shelf, occasionally holding up their phones and snapping pictures.

"I dunno…tell them you're *literally* obsessed with almond milk or quinoa or some shit?"

Evan suppressed a chuckle. "I'm serious."

"What do you want to attract tweeny somethings like that for, anyway?"

"Uh, because I want to attract paying customers."

"Well," Brian looked around. "You're about twenty years too late, man."

Evan gave him a look like he had just spoiled the end of The Sixth Sense. "Gee, thanks."

"Aw crap, I didn't mean it like that. I'm just saying, it's deader than Val Kilmer's career in here. Besides, they're just gawkers. Don't sweat it."

"You think?"

"If they actually buy something, I'll eat my own underwear."

That curious thought was cut off by none other than Mr. Panasonic offering his two cents.

Kshhhhhhhhhhhhhhhhhhhhhhhhhhhhhhhhhhhhhhhhh . . .

"Damnit," said Evan under his breath. *Of all the times!*

"What's up with that thing?" asked Brian.

Kshhhhhhhhhhhhhhhhhhhhhhhhhhhhhhhhhhhhhhhhh . . .

"It appears to be broken," Evan answered sarcastically.

Kshhhhhhhhhhhhhhhhhhhhhhhhhhhhhhhhhhhhhhhhh . . .

"Well…can you…I dunno….fix it?"

Oh gee, I hadn't thought of that. Thanks so much, buddy! You're a big help.

He hurried over to it and began fiddling with every cable connected to it to no avail. When that didn't work, he resorted to hitting it again. Which also didn't work.

BEE-BOO

"Can I help—" Evan started to say, but stopped when he saw that no one had entered...but someone had left. The two girls didn't even bother to look back.

After a few whacks the picture finally returned to show Indy surrounded by a den of snakes and Evan breathed a sigh of relief.

Something wasn't right though.

He paused the movie to be sure and pressed his ear up against the screen. It was much quieter and somehow didn't seem to be coming from behind the shield of glass, but Evan was sure he could still hear the static.

THE LINE BEGINS
TO BLUR

RAIDERS *of the Lost Ark* eventually ended and *The Never-ending Story* had begun. There hadn't been anyone else in since the two girls—at least, no one who didn't want to use the bathroom. A policy Evan was seriously re-considering since all it got him was piss on the seat and one less honey glazed. After the fourth time he went over to the gas station and confirmed his suspicions that their restroom was out of order.

That was all well and good, but they could have said thank you at least.

Brian had disappeared somewhere, the Porn Man was still puttering around behind the curtain, and the donuts were all but gone. So around the time Atreyu had reached the Southern Oracle, Evan grabbed the last cruller and retreated to the office.

A small room behind the front counter, it was stuffy, painted a horrible green color he hadn't bothered to do anything about, and home to a desk covered with bills, both opened and unopened, invoices, past due payment notices, first notices, second notices, final notices and more than a few Chinese food restaurant menus. It was also the only real place he had to keep his tool box, and behind that, a Louisville slugger in the event of intruders. But at least it was quiet.

There was nothing more to do. Nothing at all. Nothing but to wait. That was the worst.

He didn't expect customers like back in the good old Blockbuster days of yore, but there was definitely a market for VHS tapes, and other vintage film memorabilia. The question was, is that market *here*? Pondering this as he stared into space, Evan stuffed half the cruller in his mouth, covering the front of his shirt with crumbs and flakes of icing. Not even an overdose of sugar could lift his spirits.

Kshhhhhhhhhhhhhhhhhhhhhhhhhhhhhhhhhhhhhhhhh . . .

The static returned yet again. With a roll of his eyes and a long exhausted sigh, Evan hauled himself up out of the chair and went to fix it. By the time he poked his head out the office door, it had stopped. Innocently playing the end credits.

Evan narrowed his eyes and pursed his lips, skeptical. Surely he hadn't heard it before, after it disappeared from the screen earlier. It was just his mind playing tricks on him. Which is what every character plagued by an external tormentor thinks, isn't it? That they were simply mistaken or losing their mind or the classic *just imagining things*. But is that ever really how it works out?

No rising action, climax, or resolution.

That's it. That's all, folks! Thanks for coming out.

This time he didn't bother to put another movie on. Instead he let the credits run, filling the store with the movie's theme song as he returned to his seat behind the desk in his office; pausing in the doorframe for the second it took to notice the basket of tape boxes had been left in the middle of the Action Section rather than put away an hour ago like they should have been.

I could do that, he mused, itching for something to fill these empty moments and feeling the muscles of his legs tense just enough to suggest a step forward. *No. I'm not doing it for him.*

Hearing the soaring musical stylings of Limahl and Beth Anderson (and whoever actually wrote the song) made him feel a bit better. But if he was being honest with himself, not like it should.

Not like it used to.

How many times had he put on a movie he hadn't seen in years only to find it didn't hold the same magic he remembered? In some cases just the opposite. For years he held *Legend* in such high regard only to find it lacking upon viewing it as an adult. As a kid it was an escape. An adventure. Something that, while distant, seemed attainable. As an adult, he knew better. And so it instead became a sad reminder of his shattered childhood beliefs.

But he couldn't admit that. Oh no.

He maintained the facade. Held the pedestal steady as

the reverence for them became more celebrated than the thing itself, and then the reverence became fashionable, and then the fashion became common, and then the common became trivial, and then eventually the message, what they truly meant ultimately was lost in the shuffle. Wrapping paper slapped on anything by anyone at any time in order to appear as one of the tribe when really they didn't know a thing about it.

Kids who liked *Star Wars* used to be teased and taunted, called nerds and losers while today the very people who used to pick on those kids years ago all know and love "Baby Yoda". Whether this was progress or a slap in the face, Evan wasn't sure.

In that way they were not so very different from disillusioned churchgoers. They showed up, donned the clothes, repeated the lines, put on the act and all the while aware in secret that they prayed to a hollow shell of what was but too afraid to say otherwise for fear of being shunned from the temple. And if he was doing this, was it possible that everyone else who defended them so vehemently in comment sections and sub Reddits were doing exactly the same thing?

And if *that* was true…might he have built this particular temple a little too late?

Or twenty years too late, as Brian put it.

Gee, thanks.

"Yeah, thanks," he said out loud to nothing and no one.

Brian had gotten under his skin earlier, far deeper

than he cared to admit even to himself. Nothing had been meant by it, Evan knew that. Still, that didn't successfully pluck the sliver it put in his head.

But there is also more to it than that. He didn't just believe it, didn't just repeat the mantra blindly hoping to convince himself; he knew it.

These frivolous things are not all so empty.

They were an escape from overdrawn bank accounts and failed marriages. From dreams you'll never realize and co-workers whose voices you can hear in your head even when not at work.

For many, they are gospel. Scripture. Holy writ. Modern day beatitudes of far greater renown. Not to be wielded in order to lord over others and echo the same tired opinions time and again, but for anyone whose heart has ever been touched by anything to bear the name of Steven Spielberg, George Lucas, Jim Henson, or Don Bluth. He had fond memories of arcades and Nintendo. Not just digital distractions but time spent with friends. The time he spent with his dad at the drive-in or going to the video store every Friday for movie night was a ritual. Something to look forward to. Some of the happiest times he had ever had. The opening fanfare of 20th Century Fox still brought a tear to his eye every time he heard it. The quotes and references fans used weren't just facile geekery, they were a code. A lingua franca. A sign that you were in good company.

That's why these things, these fantasies, were so important. Not just to escape, but to experience.

Together. Not so we can tune out the terrible world we live in—or at least not only because of that—but to imagine what a better one would be like and make it manifest. To keep the hope alive. To see in order to believe.

He just wanted to do something that would share that with people. Was it really so crazy to think this might work? Could it be possible that he might leave something behind that would matter to someone? Even if only through sharing the works of others that had inspired him? That had given him a sense of home and comfort when it was needed.

Time will tell. Though how things went today was not a great sign.

He wanted to do so much more with his life than sit around and watch TV. Many times he had been told that he should "read more." That word: more. It implied he read at all. Aside from whatever they forced him to read in school, he couldn't think of a single book title he had chosen for himself. *Bridge to Terabithia* was the closest he got to a favorite book. That one he related to. However, he found the process of reading boring as hell and never finished it, earning a just barely passing grade on his book report. He wanted to visit places. Mexico. Japan. Thailand was supposed to be cool. But the only place he'd ever been was Disneyland many many years ago. And just like his memory of *Legend*, it was no longer quite what it used to be.

Because it doesn't work that way, does it? We can't

just abandon our responsibilities and disappear. Or pay the hefty cost of seeing and doing it all.

There was the year and a half he spent at community college taking things like Anthropology and Psych 101 for fuck knows what reason. But in the end he wound up right where he knew he would. Where he *feared* he would.

Hank's.

A soul-crushing job if ever there was one, and working with a relative too. Not just a relative, a poor excuse for a father figure to say the least. Sure, he took care of him and his mother…and never missed a chance to remind them of it. But Hank was something else. Evan hated everything about him. His puffy, over-tanned face, his golf shirts, his khakis, the stupid little smirk always on his face—snide instead of coy, the tacky pinky ring he wore on his chubby little finger. The sound of his voice with just a little hint of Texas. The fact that he was married to his mother. Everything.

That was his life, for twenty years.

He didn't ever want to *be* anything, though. Not a filmmaker, an actor, an artist, and certainly not a musician. Unlike his dad. Evan had seen what aspirations and the disappointment that followed were like, so he aimed low most of his life. Without really meaning to. Without even realizing it.

Because what would he do if he failed?

What would he do if *this* failed?

Kshhhhhhhhhhhhhhhhhhhhhhhhhhhhhhhhhhhhhhhhhh . . .

"For...fuck...sake!" Evan barked.

A split second later, the door answered.

BEE-BOO

Evan listened for the sound of Brian being useful for once today, saying those four magic words—"Can I help you?"—but all he heard was silence. He returned from behind the counter. Suddenly he didn't care that Brian wasn't there.

A woman in her early thirties maybe, wearing everyday jeans, stylish ankle boots, and a simple collared t-shirt. Brown hair with a touch of natural highlights that lacked any discernible "style," just curly and free and fit to be tossed about. If Brooke Shields had a twin sister, this would be her.

Evan straightened his shirt and tucked his hair back.

"Hello!" he said a little too high. *Reel it in a bit, stud.* Evan cleared his throat. "Can I help you?"

She slid her sunglasses down, definitely not trying to be sexy but somehow managing it anyway. Of course she would have penetrating eyes. Michelle Pfeiffer's eyes.

"I sure hope so," she said through full lips that seemed to naturally pout. "I'm looking for a VHS of *Top Gun.*"

"Yeah, no problem!" *Alright! Now we're talking,* Evan thought as he passed the Rs and Ss of the Action Section.

Beneath the curtain of the Adult Section the Porn Man's feet still shuffled aimlessly, no doubt having trouble deciding between *Good Will Humping* and *American Booty*.

Please don't let this be interrupted by him. He glared at the TV, whose electric fuzz he swore he could still hear. *Or anything else for that matter.*

Shifting his gaze back toward the shelves before him, he scanned the boxes while making his way down the alphabet. He arrived at T...

They Live...Timecop...Total Recall...Toy Soldiers... No *Top Gun.*

He thought he heard the static return and looked back toward the TV quickly. It was nowhere to be seen. Not on the screen, at least. Just the space between his ears.

Fucking Brian. He was supposed to have this done. Evan's eyes darted around as he rummaged through the basket.

"So, are you a collector?" he asked, seeing that there was no sign of it.

"Not me," said the Brooke-a-like, "but my boyfriend sure is."

"Uh-huh." Evan was only half paying attention. The other half was focused on preventing himself from giving in to an outburst building just beneath the surface.

Of all the "fucking times..." It was only then that Evan realized he was muttering to himself under his breath. Though not nearly under enough.

The static spoke up again.

Evan jerked his head as if there were an itch in the space between his ears. Impossible to scratch.

With his frustration beginning to show, the woman looked at him alertly. Nervously, even. She adjusted the strap on her purse when it was already held as close as could be.

"My fault for breaking the original, so I'm trying to find a replacement to—" Had she been able to finish the thought, the rest would have been "make up for it."

Evan halted. Slowly rose to his feet and spun to face her.

"You *broke* an original VHS copy of Top Gun?" he said with clear contempt. "Do you know how hard those are to come by today?"

Kshhhhhhhhhhhhhhhhhhhhhhhhhhhhhhhhhhhhhhhhhhh-hhhhhhhhhhhhhhhhhhhhhhhhhhhhhhhhhhhhhhhhhhhhhh . . .

And there it was. Back on the air.

"Do you have any clue?" Contempt had given way to castigation as the volume in his voice rose. She took a step back, eyes wide with alarm.

BEE-BOO

"Hey hey, what's the problem here?" said Brian, returning at last through the front door. He carried a brown paper bag from Taco Bell in one hand and a Big Gulp in the other.

Evan threw his hands up. "*There* you are!"

"Yeah, here I am," said Brian, confused. "I told you I was going to get a bite to eat. What's the—?"

"Never mind that," said Evan as he continued to search for the missing box. "Where did you put *Top Gun*??"

BEE-BOO

There was just enough time to see Brooke disappear through the door before it slammed behind her. The sign above reminded him to BE KIND, but it was too late. She definitely wouldn't be returning.

Evan threw up his hands again. "That's great. That's *just* great!"

"Will you chill out, man? Seriously. And why are you yelling?"

Kshhhhhhhhhhhhhhhhhhhhhhhhhhhhhhhhhhhhhhhhhh-hhhhhhhhhhhhhhhhhhhhhhhh . . .

"Can you *not* hear that?"

Brian stepped quickly over to the TV, "Did you ever think to try this?" and turned down the volume. "There. Much better."

Only it wasn't. Evan still heard it at exactly the same volume.

"You were supposed to put the rest of the fucking Action Section away, Brian!" Evan yelled as if over a terrible racket.

"Whoa! Let's check the aggression, man."

"Don't tell me to check anything," said Evan with a point of his finger. "I'm *your* boss!"

Now it was Brian's turn to shoot him a look, one that said he'd been told that *Firefly* is overrated. "You know what, I don't need this shit."

"Meaning what?"

"I don't need this job." Brian angrily pulled the

REWIND VIDEO shirt off over his head and threw it to the floor. "I'm out."

"Yeah you're right, cramps your usual routine of toking and jerking off."

Shirtless, Brian made for the door, shoved it open and flipped him off as he left.

BEE-BOO

"Fine! Go ahead. You'll be back."

Hank's words coming out of *his* mouth.

A moment later—*BEE-BOO*—he saw that he was right. Brian marched back in without a word or even so much as eye contact, went to the back and reappeared wearing the shirt he had entered with earlier that day.

BEE-BOO

Then he flipped him off again.

Kshhhhhhhhhhhhhhhhhhhhhhhhhhhhhhhhhhhhhhh . . .

Evan unplugged the TV, cutting the picture altogether and hauled it from its cozy corner of the front counter. So mad, fuming even, that he hardly even noticed the weight. Leaving the cord to rattle along the ground behind him, Evan kicked the door to the office in and plunked it down on the desk, displacing more than a few layers of paper from the mound atop it.

His hand was on the doorknob, ready to leave—ready not to give it another moment's thought.

Kshhhhhhhhhhhhhhhhhhhhhhhhhhhhhhhhhhhhhhh . . .

He slowly turned.

Kshhhhhhhhhhhhhhhhhhhhhhhhhhhhhhhhhhhhhhh . . .

Stared at it.

The cathode spat distortion at him, inside and out, as the plug dangled off one side of the desk, a foot and a half at least from so much as touching the nearest outlet. Hesitating for a moment, he slammed the door shut and grabbed his keys from under the front counter. The hell with the fact that it was nowhere near closing time. He had to get away from here.

Evan left the store and locked up. No more than two feet from the door there came the gentle tap of plastic on glass behind him.

He turned to see the Porn Man still inside.

"I'll take this one." His voice muffled as he held up a charming little flick called *Saturday Night Beaver*.

SOMETHING I CAN NEVER HAVE

ALL THE WAY to the liquor store, Evan could hear that static. Not on full blast like before. Below the surface. Between the sounds of the city. Flowing beneath each song on the radio like a deep sea current. He saw it in the traffic lights, in the store windows, in the eyes of the clerk as she rang up his six pack and said, "Have a nice day."

Even when he closed his eyes, it was there. Singed into his retinas like the afterimage of a camera flash that wasn't going away. After he got his beer and a pizza from the place next door, he didn't want to go back. But sitting in his van and eating it in a strip mall parking lot was just a little too pathetic even for him. If he returned to see the unplugged television crackling with static when it shouldn't be...if that was something he had to face...

Surely that can't have been what happened, right?... "I am sure. And don't call me Shirley"...

There's got to be a perfectly logical explanation. There has to be…

Still…it didn't occur to him at the time but…it shouldn't have turned to static just because the cables weren't plugged in. But then, it also shouldn't have been fixed by hitting it a few times. That only works on TV.

ON TV.

How could that happen? Like, seriously how?

The truth was that it couldn't.

Oh god. Am I losing my mind?…And there it is! *Cliché complete. Terrific.*

On the way back, Evan caught the familiar glow of neon and auto-filled the letters around it to that of his store. The one thing he could admire and feel proud to have achieved.

Only it was four blocks too soon.

Instead it was that of another store: RETRO VIDEO. It looked like his, felt like his, but was in a better location and doing better business than his. A lot better. The place wasn't packed but there were people inside; people who weren't there to just use the bathroom or look for porn. It was tough to get a full view of the place from the street, but it appeared that a curtained Adult Section was the one thing missing from RETRO VIDEO. Making it a different kind of place.

A family place.

Just four fucking blocks away.

And with that particular penny dropped, his heart fell with it.

31

Evan didn't need to have a porn section. He didn't even necessarily want one. He was just trying to make his store the way he remembered them. The way they had been. Authentic. Real. In a way he was sure others would get and remember as well. Even appreciate.

Now he wasn't so sure.

So there he sat in his van, watching through the brightly lit store window that said OPEN on the sign. To him, it couldn't have been more closed.

A wrong and wrathful white bloomed in every knuckle as his grip tightened on the steering wheel, as though the bones beneath might break the skin. In that moment he wanted things to be suffering, living the same moment of numb anger he was.

He wanted to break every smiling face.

He wanted to make things bleed.

The static became a force of its own. A most hateful of winters. Intense and abrasive to the point that silence would suddenly feel foreign. And there it stayed until he returned to the store.

BEE-BOO

He was getting really tired of that sound already. More than tired. This time his chest tightened and a longer than usual inward breath was needed to get further than one step inside.

Evan strode past the office, not bothering to so much

as look in the direction of the closed door, and to the second floor he went. And in doing so only wedged his fear of what he might find behind it even deeper.

The room upstairs should have been for people to have lunch or grab coffee. Now, it was home. Two hundred square feet or so of open space with a kitchenette, a fridge and even a dishwasher. No shower though. For that he had to use the one at the gym, and be a little less particular about how frequently he could have one. There was a stained futon at one end, a chipped night stand next to it with an extension lamp on top, and against the wall was the same plasma flat screen he'd had for the last decade. As far as earthly possessions went that was about it. The walls were covered with movie posters and piled up with boxes that hadn't been unpacked because there was nowhere to put their contents. It had a funky smell to it, like someone's old grilled cheese had fallen behind one of the appliances and was never retrieved if only to be given a proper burial in the trash.

Everything about the place cried, *It'll do.*

Or more like, *It'll* have *to do.*

But it didn't matter. If it meant making the store happen, anything was worth it.

Right?

After dropping his wallet and keys on the counter, Evan greeted the one other resident of this most humble of abodes—his pet turtle Leo, currently chomping away on a thick piece of lettuce in his tank next to the sink. Content as a turtle could be. And in that moment, he envied the life of a reptile.

Evan stuck the beer in the fridge but not before cracking one can of Pilsner and draining it in a few gulps, turning a six pack into five.

Dirty dishes took up every bit of space in the sink. No reason why with a dishwasher. All he had to do was put them in and turn it on. But he hadn't. His clothes were heaped in another pile strewn between the boxes they came in and a hamper that was brimming over with laundry that needed to be done. He just…didn't.

Evan brought the pizza and another beer over to the futon and slumped down into it. He clicked on the TV and began flipping through the channels as he thought long and hard over everything that had happened today. This, he reminded himself, was the cost of dreams. Of following your bliss. Was it always smooth? No. You do it because you love it.

Then why doesn't this feel blissful?

What if this labor of love becomes too costly? To a point that I can't do it anymore or run the risk of going bankrupt. A penniless peasant. A bum. A loser. If I'm not already.

Like Dad.

He hated himself a little for thinking that, he knew it was wrong, but the truth was that a part of him never forgave his dad for leaving him. Of course that wasn't exactly what happened. He didn't "leave." That's just how it felt. And that's how it was for a long time. Years. Later, when he could bring himself to look into such things, he learned how people who commit suicide suffer. It's not cowardly or weak. It's a lack of options. A desire to end the suffering. He didn't realize it at the time, but looking back he could tell that his dad had suffered. From depression, addiction, defeat in the pursuit of his own dreams, you name it. He had no idea as a kid. None. His dad always seemed like a happy guy. Smiled a lot, laughed a lot, joked around a lot. Maybe a little too much. A little too often. Only in adulthood did he realize that not every one who appears happy on the outside truly is. It's just a mask they wear to cover up how they feel inside. Until they can't anymore.

Evan vowed never to go that route. No matter how hard things got, he would stay above ground. Because then there's a chance.

But is that worth it? Am I doomed to go crawling back, tail tucked between my legs, to where I started? Broke and broken? At what point do I throw in the towel and just agree to be the same joyless, soul-crushed person as everyone else. Taxidermied into wooden smiles giving some semblance of life on the surface while blood fights to pump through my veins. Surviving but not really living.

Maybe not yet. Today was just one day.

But what about the next day?

And the day after that?

And the day after that?

If this didn't work, if this wasn't worth everything he put into it, then it was all for nothing.

He'd have to close the store, and with nowhere to go and financially destitute, he would wind up living in his van. Somehow he doubted that he'd be welcome to move back home, and even if he was, he wouldn't want to. However that went, the balance of his life would be empty.

Alone.

Evan cracked the beer can open and poured nearly half of it down his throat.

We're all just children of a dying age. Raised by fictional characters, instilled with the morals and messages of after school specials, taught love and friendship and warmth by the families of sitcoms rather than our own. Planned our week around the programming of the TV Guide. And for what? To be able to look back and say there was a better time, and how sad it is that things today aren't like they were then? Every decade that passes, the fewer people there are that remember those times. We cling to our memory of them more dearly than the real thing. Because to us they are more real than reality.

Because reality is a terrible thing.

Our ancestors used to gather around a fire to tell stories, we've just replaced the hearth with the nearest screen. We peer into each one as if they were crystal balls in which we'll find the answers we seek. Television was blamed for making the general population more violent and detached. But the truth is that people have always been that way. TV merely gave us another thing to obsess over. Another way to indulge. We make our entertainment that way because it's already in us, not the other way around. We may want to be good, we may be interested in it, we may even manage to make some progress once in a while. But what we excel at is anything but good. Self-destruction, disgust, disease, degradation, and indifference. That's where our talents truly lie. It's our default. And deep down we know this.

We fear it.

Good does not triumph over evil, love does not conquer all, and not everything works out in the end. In this world, Will Hunting continues to mop the floors of MIT, never knows what could have been, and dies a lonely, bitter man. E.T. never returns home and winds up dissected in some secret government experiment. Bender returns with his dad's gun and kills the rest of the Breakfast Club. Sarah Conner is terminated on the first try, and all hope for humanity along with her. The Empire prevails. Biff rapes Marty's mom. And no dogs go to Heaven. That's *the world we live in.*

Viewer depression advised.

It was enough to make Evan want to sit and eat an entire pizza to himself. And so he did.

He looked at his place, his home, his dragon's lair of geek treasure. Relics of that dying age he had spent his whole life collecting. *Is this it? Is this what my life is? Is this all it's going to be? Is this my legacy? This den of limited edition cheap plastic and resin among dirty dishes, unwashed clothes, and bills.*

Evan saw down the road to the future, and sadly it wasn't that far at all. What more might he be able to count on for certain? Another thirty years? After that, it's a coin toss. And considering his lifestyle and risk factors, perhaps even less. Every time a hemorrhoid bled, he feared it was cancer. Same with any time he felt tired, or didn't have an appetite, or got a headache. All things with benign reasons behind them…but one time, just one time was all it took.

And it could be the next one.

Finally, on some future date he couldn't predict, he saw himself clutching his chest as the clogged arteries of his heart choked him from the inside out, and dying.

Then what?

Pearly gates? Paradise? Seeing all my loved ones again, elevated to some higher form of existence, free to explore and know the mysteries of the cosmos?

Nah. Life isn't so convenient, why should death be any different? Everything that exists truly, naturally, comes in pairs—light and dark, day and night, hot and cold. So when you consider that life is order, presence, consciousness, awareness of self and senses, interaction and effect on our environment, it follows that death would then be the inverse. A lack of all these things.

Nothingness.

We can't even comprehend it. Nonexistence is a complete and utter non sequitur to us. As invention is the product of necessity, the idea of an afterlife sprung from our need to stave off the cold reality of an even colder fact—we don't go on. And we're forgotten far too soon and too easily, even for those who knew us. One day we're just...gone.

What then for the rest of the world? Will they learn to treat the earth better? To treat each other better? To treat themselves better?

The irony of pondering this as he plucked another piece of pizza from its cardboard box, clogging up his heart and the environment in one swoop after a day in which he angrily drove off everyone he came into contact was not lost on him. He drained the last of his beer, crushed the can with his fist and chucked it at the wall.

Doubtful. Not impossible, but doubtful. Humanity's track record with hearing the train well before it bore down on us left something to be desired. In the end we're no different from any other species who have gone as far as they can—or in this case, as far as we're willing to go. Superior to nothing.

What then is the destiny of this world? That every forest should be replaced by shopping malls, every tree by smoke stacks, and every river by freeways? We trivialize these things because they exist only in part. But considering that the goal is to have as much of them as possible—or what is rapidly becoming as much as is necessary to sustain an ever-growing population—the conclusion is terrifying. Everything around us is fake. And all of that is doomed to the same fate. It's a path we all eventually follow. One way or another. Life kills us all.

Unless we can leave something that will remain. Isn't that what we're told?

But why should we be special? Any of us. Even the things we leave behind will eventually be gone one day too. It's inevitable. From every kindergarten finger painting to the Mona Lisa, everything eventually ends up on the trash heap. No matter how powerful, beautiful, or important. No matter how poignant, how revered by a respected critic or how central to the aims and principles of society, culture, and civilization, none of it lasts forever.

Why should that be so bad? We equate the negativity of death with the lack of our presence, but how stressed are the dinosaurs today? How worried about its cholesterol is a dodo or great auk? Does an aborted fetus have to fret over what people think about them? What does Aristotle have to say about the meaning of life right now? How much easier would it be if a meteor took us all out? Sure, there'd be some moaning and crying about it beforehand but afterward, it would be pretty peaceful.

The truth is that we're the same matter as anything

else. Meat that nature saw fit to curse with a mind. Not just able to fear death, but also dread its certainty. We know for whom the bell tolls but not how long it will be before we hear it ourselves.

There was one thing he was sure of though: it's too soon. Whether you live to nine or ninety, that tempus fugits without mercy. Here one moment, gone the next.

Fade to black.

THE END

No question mark.

Of course there was always the having kids option. That's a way to leave something behind. One Evan may have even wanted too. At some point. Someone he could watch Star Wars with. Teach how to throw a football. How to drive. How to shave. Be what his dad was to him...for a while, at least. But of course for that you need a woman.

"I don't want to have your baby."

Her words, still so clear like shrapnel in a wound that can't be touched without doing further damage. He and Jenny were good together at first, when nothing mattered but sex and fun. They didn't have to worry about planning or the future or anything at all. Then as time went on, how little they had in common became impossible to ignore. He liked movies, she didn't. She liked country music, he didn't. He wanted a family, she didn't...at least not with him. That was one thing he never got really clear on—whether she didn't want to have a family at all or just didn't want to with him.

After that, things slowly fell apart. Bit by bit. That was a year ago now. . .

No, two.

He spent every day since rewinding and replaying those words in his head. In many ways the end of a relationship is a loss. But the thing he mourned the most was the loss not of Jenny from his life, but the possibility she represented.

The loss of hope.

Something good did come of it, though. If it wasn't for that, he wouldn't have realized how short life was and started REWIND VIDEO.

Yeah, and look how that's going.

Right on cue, the sitcom's laugh track interrupted. Not that he was really paying attention to it anyway. He had just flipped through the channels until he found something tolerable that might lift his spirits with some light, albeit mediocre, comedy. With his mind in the gutter—not in the good way—it was hard to see as anything but an inane farce. A poor excuse for entertainment rife with safe jokes and bad writing. Families smiling, eating dinner together, laughing. The only time he ate with his mom and Hank was birthdays, Thanksgiving, or Christmas. And considering that they were three people with not a lot in common or reason to be together otherwise, they were pretty awkward meals. No one would watch that show.

He couldn't help but wonder how it might go if portrayed more realistically...

[Cue intro music]

DAD
Hi, honey! I'm home.

MOM
How was your day?

DAD
Great! I just fucked my secretary before leaving work.

[Cue laughter]

MOM
Swell! Give her my regards. Speaking of which, I'm pregnant.

[AWWW]

DAD
Is it mine?

MOM
Oh not even close!

43

[Cue laughter]

                    DAD
        Darn. Say, where are the kids?

                    MOM
    Well, Junior is down in the basement
        working on his science project.

                    DAD
    Ah. What is it today? Cooking meth or
        dissolving dead animals in acid?

                    MOM
    Judging by the smell, a bit of both.

[Cue laughter]

                    DAD
        Oh that Junior. And our daughter?

                    MOM
    Nursing an eating disorder, so she
    won't be joining us for dinner. Oh and
            she's pregnant too!

                    DAD
        Fantastic! Who's the father?

                        MOM
              Your brother, Jack!

        [Cue laughter]

                        DAD
                      Terrific!

        Enter JANET the secretary.

                       JANET
        Guess what, Boss? I'm pregnant too!

        [Cue laughter]

Evan was snapped out of the scenario by a sudden bump
on the wall his back was against. Not loud, but enough to
surprise him. He had no clue what had made it. That was
the first time he had realized something that should have
occurred to him long before, except that he had no reason
to until now—on the other side of that wall there were
other people. He imagined others in the spaces between
them sitting stock still and stunned, staring into space,
disassociated, thinking similarly grim thoughts. No more
between them than a few inches of plaster and fiberglass
insulation, yet somehow this made him feel more alone
than ever.

    Evan slid his phone out from his pocket. A tap of his

thumb and his brain went numb, lost in the feed of one app or another the instant he hit the icon. He didn't care about most of this shit—pictures of people's food, pictures of people's vacations, pictures of people's kids, and the facile comments attached to each one.

Happy Friday!

You look great.

Get well soon.

Thinking of you.

Congrats!

OMG

LOL

All inter-spliced with war, tragedy, disease, murder, racism, and all manner of real world horrors he felt powerless to affect.

Thoughts and prayers.

Buy this! Buy that! Buy EVERYTHING!

Add To Cart

He only scrolled through it all hoping he might spot something worth seeing, a movie trailer that had just dropped or the like. Something to give him any small semblance of joy. Instead it just clouded his head further.

Without meaning to, like so many things on social media, he searched for the account he created for REWIND VIDEO. Not something he relished having to do, but these days if you don't have an online presence, you may as well not exist.

There was nothing.

No comments, no notifications, no new views, no one who had seen the store and felt touched knowing that this little sliver of a simpler time exists. At this point he would have even welcomed a troll, someone telling him to get with the times, that no one would visit such a place because movies were all done through streaming now. Someone criticizing *Rambo* for its pro-war stance or *The Phantom Menace* for ruining their childhood. At least that would be something.

But no.

Silence.

We've become each other's Big Brother. Who's watching who? And who's not watching? Maybe it's always been this way. How would the Salem witch trials have gone if Twitter was around in 1692? Or the Cold War. Or even 9/11. Never mind warriors, we've become keyboard guerrillas. Keyboard spies. Keyboard assassins. Keyboard sleeper agents. Keyboard cultists. Keyboard extremists. Keyboard predators. Our arsenal is one of memes and gifs and ALL CAPS. Our flags are hashtags. Everyone's got their finger on the trigger, and today it was too hard to tell a good guy with a cause from a bad guy with a cause.

The "media" used to be paparazzi, tabloids, news outlets all clambering after the next bit of gossip for our entertainment, and in some cases, our distraction. Now the public are *the media. Both creating and reporting the news. There's no line to cross anymore. No longer content merely to watch; we are part of the circus now. We were given the means to be their eyes and ears and we said yes please faster than it takes to post a picture of your sushi to Instagram. Only we decided that celebrities weren't the only fair game anymore, opting to turn the lens on each other. And when that wasn't available, we turn it on ourselves. Mainlining the attention our manufactured personas reap from organically grown followings. Squeezing out every ounce of serotonin until we need a higher dose and have to go further and further to get it. Go big. Go viral. All of which just leads to the same thing—noise.*

It was the main reason Evan tried to stay offline as much as possible. To avoid the racket. The silence was the other reason. He heard every silence. Noticed every absence. When it mattered, it was louder than any sound ever could be, but not loud enough to drown out the repetitive thought: *What's wrong with me? What am I doing wrong?*

But like so many things, it could be used for good or ill. Just as a hammer is a tool in one pair of hands and a weapon in others. He had seen good done with it. Old friends meeting after a long time. Risks taken, ventures braved, and connections made. Romances kindled. He had seen complete strangers on the internet engage in the most touching acts of kindness and compassion for other strangers who had no one in their "real" life.

He just wasn't one of them.

The canned laughter from the TV mocked him.

"That's enough of that," he said, and turned it off.

And as he sat there, weighed down and numbed by so much baggage, Evan swore that he could still hear that fucking static!

Kshhhhhhhhhhhhhhhhhhhhhhhhhhhhhhhhhhhhhh . . .

Impossible. He was nowhere near it. But he could. Clear as could be.

Evan turned the TV back on to drown it out.

Kshhhhhhhhhhhhhhhhhhhhhhhhhhhhhhhhhhhhhh . . .

It was there now too.

"NO!" he ranted. "Not possible!"

Forcing himself up, he grabbed his keys from the counter and hurried all the way downstairs back to the store.

Evan flung the door to the office open. The TV was just how he had left it. Cord dangling off the desk. Crackling, erratic, intrusive gray noise.

Kshhhhhhhhhhhhhhhhhhhhhhhhhhhhhhhhhhhhhh . . .

So loud there was a rattle to it now.

He left just long enough to prop open the front door, then returned to hoist it up into his arms. With the distorted signal behind the glass pressed right against his chest, he marched outside and tossed it into the dumpster across the lot. Surprising the hell out of a stray cat in the process as it leapt out and ran away.

Each step he took away from it, the static grew louder until it was almost deafening.

The blue glow of the screen that was still on, despite having no possible way to be, peeked out from over the rim, just a small corner of it. Filled by static.

Back he went to the dumpster, hauled it out by the cord left dangling again over the rim and tumbled down to the hard concrete ground. It didn't show so much as a crack.

Evan dragged the TV by the cord, scraping it along the pavement—garnering bewildered stares from a man filling up his pickup truck at the pumps—until it was back inside the store.

The sheer volume of it cast radial waves of pain in his ears and eye sockets. Sound and feeling merged into a single sensation, plaguing him like a swarm of electric bees.

He smacked it like he had before, trying to knock the reception clear, to no avail.

He smacked his head, trying to knock himself out. Wishing for it. Begging for it.

Gritting his teeth so hard that he felt them bend at the root, Evan hurried into the office and returned with the slugger. The fucking thing had to die! He wound back over his shoulder and brought the bat down as hard as he could. A blinding white hit him as the blow he dealt the TV struck his skull simultaneously.

He got his wish.

———

Kshhhhhhhhhhhhhhhhhhhhhhhhhhhhhhhhhhhhhhhhhhhhhh-
hhhhhhhhhhhhhhhhhhhhhhhhhhhhhhhhhhhhhhhhhhhhhhhh

This sound.

hhhhhhhhhhhhhhhhhhhhhhhhhhhhhhhhhhhhhhhhhhhhhhh-
hhhhhhhhhhhhhhhhhhhhhhhhhhhhhhhhhhhhhhhhhhhhhhhh

Even in the deep unconscious places of his mind,

hhhhhhhhhhhhhhhhhhhhhhhhhhhhhhhhhhhhhhhhhhhhhhh-
hhhhhhhhhhhhhhhhhhhhhhhhhhhhhhhhhhhhhhhhhhhhhhhh

where such frequencies should not be able to reach,

hhhhhhhhhhhhhhhhhhhhhhhhhhhhhhhhhhhhhhhhhhhhhhh-
hhhhhhhhhhhhhhhhhhhhhhhhhhhhhhhhhhhhhhhhhhhhhhhh

this sound.

hhhhhhhhhhhhhhhhhhhhhhhhhhhhhhhhhhhhhhhhhhhhhhh-
hhhhhhhhhhhhhhhhhhhhhhhhhhhhhhhhhhhhhhhhhhhhhhhh . . .

———

When Evan awoke, the static had not only remained at full volume but was now joined by a high-pitched tone. Shrill like a test of the Emergency Broadcast System only unbroken. Relentless.

He crawled on all fours until he reached the counter, using it to pull himself up, drooling like his prefrontal cortex had been mashed in with the pain to match it.

Please god, STOP! Evan shouted internally, drowned out over the noise.

On his feet again, a blurred gaze steadied and settled on the desk of his office and the open toolbox next to it.

There was the drill.

No thought. It wasn't possible with the level of noise surging through every bend and groove of his gray matter. No time for fear or remorse. No time for his life to flash before his eyes. It was the one small mercy he was afforded.

Like the shoddy camera work of a found footage film, his vision shook as he staggered forward. Evan grabbed the drill, pinched his eyes shut as hard as he could and squeezed the button. The eager drill bit, left to sit and wait for far too long, instantly spun and with it came the buzz of rotating gears.

Kshhhhhhhhhhhhhhhhhhhhhhhhhhhhhhhhhhhhhhhhhh-hhhhhhhhhhhhhhhhhhhhhhhhhhhhhhhhhhhhhhhhhhhhh . . .

He inched the whirring metal closer and closer to his right temple.

JUST MAKE IT STOP!

The screen sputtered.

Brief as could be, but for a split second there had been a break in the static.

Evan released his grip on the drill and returned to the TV.

Around the screen, an odd glow emitted. Ugly. Sunken. A light that would cause things to wither rather than grow. A light that gave no warmth but instead stole it. He was drawn toward it like a moth to the most unnatural of flames. The box itself showed almost no light as if it were afraid to tread too heavily upon it. Every photon absorbed so that even the metallic letters that spelled Panasonic no longer reflected. Anything that dared to shine was consumed. Sucked in and trapped like a miniature black hole. Unable to escape.

The fluorescent bulbs above flickered in unison with whatever abnormal signal was coming through. A shadow began to leak from the bottom of the TV. Spreading across the floor in a mass of pixelated tendrils and frayed wires. Up the nearby counter. Up the walls. A penumbra of soiled, dirty light preceded everything it touched. Casting its shaded guise as it fell upon each part of the store. Making the wire racks rust. The faces of each actor turned into dead, gray corpses of themselves as the cardboard boxes upon them crumbled. A thick layer of ash from whatever crematory matter remains after death settled upon it all as the shadow spread across the ceiling, rendering the overhead light fixtures null. Swallowing everything visible around it until there was just a square of light in a pitch black like no other.

Evan stared at the screen, willed it to do something. Say something. Give him anything other than this ceaseless droning.

He peered into it.

Beyond it.

Disconnected with the body that chained him to existence and was lost in the void between chaotic points of light. Beguiled by oblivion. Darkness unending. Not even darkness; that would imply an absence of light. Not life or death. This was neither.

This was the Abyss itself.

It was then that he knew this instrument, crude though it may be, was both its vessel and its prison. The antithesis of being. A point of nothing. A vacuole of the negative. A fledgling of the void. A window through which it could peer into the material world. This was no herald. No hierophant. No being called by one name or another. Such things were the custom of the corporeal, and therefore beneath it. Only able to influence this reality by debasing itself in becoming manifest, siphoning from it that which it needs to subsist. Attempting to grasp how it had arrived on this plane of existence made his mind unreel.

How ludicrous he suddenly found it all. How needlessly complicated and unnecessary the very fact that he existed. That *anything* existed. Offensive, even. Where once there had only been the great unknowable therebefore, one day he was forced squalling and repulsive into the material world.

No consent. No agency. No choice.

Eating, bathing, shitting, aging, dry lips, acne, cavities, ulcers. How wonderful would it be to be rid of it all? All matter that anchored his physical self no longer meant anything, and for one perfect instant, he was free.

Darkness seems so empty sometimes. But if you stop and look, really look where there's no light, you'll see that it's anything but. It's the very fabric from which we make our own terrors. Manifest every face and form and nightmare we refuse to look at but can't ignore. It's only when we peer into darkness that we realize that the horror isn't out there.

It's in us.

Shapes became clear in the static. A picture. Whether real or some form of pareidolia, in it he saw a winding pattern. Lines and passages. A maze or topographical map or the deepest penetralia of some long forgotten city. As the lines gradually darkened, not a maze but rather a tightly packed trail of intestines appeared, practically bulging out of the screen. Riddled with polyps and open sores. Seeping with blood, stomach acids, puss, and all manner of bodily fluids. At the same time a sharp foreign pain appeared in his abdomen, shredding at him from the inside, as if his guts had been replaced by a heap of unspooled videotape.

He blinked.

The store returned to normal.

But the static remained.

Kshhhhhhhhhhhhhhhhhhhhhhhhhhhhhhhhhhhhhhhhhh-hhhhhhhhhhhhhhhhhhhhhhhhhhhhhhhh . . .

Evan got down on his knees and clamped the TV with his hands on either side. "What do you want?!" he shouted, nose pressed to the screen.

The static ceased immediately.

The screen went solid black.

For a moment he thought it had shut off.

One remaining pixel was left on. A single point that slowly but clearly began to grow bigger; expanding until it filled the screen and replaced the black with a dark hallway. One he recognized.

Nothing happened for a few moments . . .

Then a person appeared at the other end.

It was Hank. Walking through the upstairs of the hardware store to his office.

How he was seeing this, Evan had no clue. There was no way a security camera feed could be received all that way. The image just stayed on him as he went into his office at the end of the hall, then suddenly drifted forward like the camera had detached and floated through the air to follow. It showed Hank sitting at his desk, doing paperwork with ESPN on in the background. Unaware that we was being watched.

"Okay," said Evan, expecting something else to come next.

It didn't.

"What do you want me to do?" Even as he asked the

question, he both knew and feared what might come next. An answer he knew like a shiver from the cold.

The screen went red. Pure red. Bled into every pixel. Stayed solid for a moment before washing away in a torrent of blood, followed by a chorus of screams as a montage flashed raggedly across the screen in spurts of chopped and spliced film.

Jason's empty eyes and machete . . . Freddy's clawed hand and wicked smile . . . The merciless buzz of Leatherface's chainsaw . . . Ghostface driving a buck knife through one victim after another . . . Marion Crane stabbed again and again and again and again in the shower . . . Candyman splitting people from groin to gullet . . . Michael Meyers pinning a poor sap to the wall behind him, admiring his work . . . Carrie White soaked in blood, burning each and every person at the prom to a crisp . . . The elevator door of the Overlook Hotel opening up and spilling a gigantic wave of blood.

REDRUM

"No."

REDRUM

"I can't."

REDRUM

Can I?

The screen went silent again.

Then...

Kshhhhhhhhhhhhhhhhhhhhhhhhhhhhhhhhhhhhhhh . . .

Full force. Louder than it had ever been. Louder than

should have been possible. Loud enough to show that it had only been toying with him before now.

It overtook him.

A thousand garbled points pressing into his brain from all angles.

"Stop!" he shouted, out of breath. The very rim of his sanity blistered and fried to a point of overload. Defeat sunk in and hardened like rapidly drying cement. "I'll do it."

WE'RE IN THIS TOGETHER

EVAN SAT in his van staring at the entrance of Hank's Hardware, the noise in his head quieter than before but constant, wincing at the ever-lasting tone that now came with it. He waited until he had the full cover of night on his side, when the summer dusk had disappeared completely. The drive there was something he had done so many times it barely required any navigation at all. Which was fortunate since the static precluded the possibility of linear thought...except for one...

If I just hadn't picked up that stupid TV . . .

Normally there would be a bustling store front with people driving back and forth, loading things into one vehicle or unloading them from another before him. Now it was deserted. Every window, dark and empty. All but one, where a blue light flickered in the glass of a second floor office. Hank often worked late, making that the one thing about this which was not out of the ordinary.

The noise increased in volume, an incessant, splintering wedge driving deeper and deeper, insisting he get on with his task. Winding tightly between each scrambled point. His jaw hurt from clenching it so hard. His hands were sore from gripping the wheel so tight.

In the passenger's seat, a crowbar lay waiting. Another thing he didn't have a choice in—how he would actually kill Hank. He didn't own a gun, didn't have any non-plastic cutlery and certainly not a cleaver. Didn't even have any bungee cord that he might strangle him with. In a pinch he could easily dispose of the crowbar. Clumsy, but more than capable of doing the job. A hammer might have been better but he had lent his to Brian and never got it back.

Looking around cautiously to make sure the coast was clear, that there were no faces present in the night, Evan got out—careful not to let the door slam shut—and headed for the store.

The nearer he got the softer the static became. Not in volume but gentler. More forgiving.

Kshhhhhhhhhhhhhhhhhhhhhhhhhhhhh That's right shhh-hhhhhhhhhhhhhhh You are shhhhhhhhhhhhhhhhhhhhh getting shhhhhhhhhhhhhhhhhhhhhh warmer shhhhhhhhhhh-hhhhhhhhhhh . . .

He knew the back way in was his best bet. Darker, more cover. Still, there was one security camera, but that was a problem he would have to deal with once inside.

And therein was the real trick.

Unlike the front, that opened with good old fashioned metal-as-fuck keys, which he had turned in when he quit, the back door was controlled with an electronic lock. And that was opened with a card reader operated by an ID pass. That he still had. Having pulled it from around his neck and dropped to the floor of his van when he left, it had been left there happily forgotten until now.

There was a chance—a slim one, but a chance—that it might not have been deactivated.

If it had, there would be another use for the crowbar.

Evan lifted the card toward the reader, palms sweating, as his chest clamped up waiting to see what would happen.

The static whispered a bit louder but for once, not at him.

The little red light on the reader blinked green before he could even swipe it.

He stood there, aghast. With a last quick look around, he pulled the door open and let himself in as quietly as he could.

Evan made for the staircase that led to the second floor where the break room, meeting room, and Hank's office were. Up there was the key to his salvation. Passing a pair of batwing doors he took a step back and nudged one side open just a crack to get a look at the empty store.

The most liminal of spaces. Aisle upon aisle of power tools glinting in what light shone through the window outside. Mowers, nails, drill bits, bags of sawdust and all manner of other things, but not another living soul. Something about seeing somewhere normally filled with people completely devoid of them does something to the mind. A mind which abhors blanks and empty spaces. One which cannot truly ever know silence.

Kshhhhhhhhhhhhhhhhhhhhhhhhhhh get on with it shhhhhhhhhhhhhhhhhhhhhhhhhhhhhhhhhhhhhhhhhhhhh-hhhhhhhhhhhhhhhhhhhhhhhhhhhhhhhhhh

Speaking of which.

God how he needed it to stop. Didn't even care about getting caught anymore. A prison cell would be a welcome respite. Who knows? Maybe when he tells them that a TV made him do it he'll get sent to a nice cozy asylum. Three meals a day, arts and crafts, meds, ping pong. He might have to deal with ball-busting orderlies and a bunk mate who liked to watch him sleep, but if it all came with silence, then it was worth it.

Assuming it did come with silence. What if this wasn't it? What if he wound up seeing the static in the eyes and scrambled faces of the other patients and nurses, trapped in there with him with nowhere else to go? What if the noise demanded more blood?

Up the staircase he went. Carefully lifting each foot and placing it down softly so as not to make a sound on the metal of each step. The static eased again the nearer he got, but his conscience did not.

You're about to kill somebody.

His whole head ached. The spot between his eyes splitting like the tip of a nail being slowly pressed into his skull.

He's an asshole. He made me feel like I was a guest

*in my own home. Even said as much. He was impossible
to please. I could never do anything right by him. He hit
me. Made me walk on eggshells. Made me feel like I
should be less like me and more like him. Fell back on
the old "back in my day" and "when I was your age"
and "what my old man used to do" to justify things.*

And every time, for every one of those things, he
wanted to kill him. Or at least wanted him to die. Be
gone. Be out of his life. Out of his mother's life. She was
a good woman and he loved her, but when it came to
Hank she was a total pushover. He didn't hate her; he
hated who she was around him. *Because* of him.

But had he ever thought about doing it? Actually
doing it?

Not until now.

At the top of the stairs Evan looked up to the security
camera near the ceiling, the one placed at the end of the
hall. The one whose feed had shown up on the TV in his
store. He could just make out the glass eye of the lens. It
was filled with static.

Down the hall he went, past the break room, as
stealthily as he could. The sound of Sports Centre blared
out of the open door, followed by bursts of blue light of
whatever was flashing across the screen.

There was some movement from within Hank's
office.

Evan froze.

It sounded like he had got up from his swivel chair,
but there were no steps.

After a few tense moments, the leather squelched as Hank sat back down.

Evan closed the distance.

The door to Hank's office was wide open, and thanks to a framed picture on the wall across the hall from it he could just make out his reflection. Bald head. Golf shirt. Hairy arms. The glow of the television across the room flickering. He was facing the open door, meaning there was no way to sneak up on him.

Just then Neil Everett's voice was cut off while talking about the Pats' recent loss to Green Bay.

Kshhhhhhhhhhhhhhhhhhhhhhhhhhhhhhhhhhhhhhhhhh-hhhhhhhhhhhhhhhhhhhhhhhhhhhhhhh . . .

"Damn it," said Hank as he got up from his desk to fix the problem. A few quick steps and he was there.

Right there.

Just on the other side of the door.

Evan smacked his head. Tried to knock the reception clear to no avail. The static was twofold now. Both inside and out. Waxing to some horrible point of deafness that never came.

Kshhhhhhhhhhhhhhhhhhhhhhhhhh . . .

A roaring gray abyss.

Kshhhhhhhhhhhhhhhhhhhhhhhhhh . . .

Gulfs of ceaseless sound.

Kshhhhhhhhhhhhhhhhhhhhhhhhhh . . .

Volume beyond sense.

Kshhhhhhhhhhhhhhhhhhhhhhhhhh . . .

A discordant nightmare of monochromatic haze.

Kshhhhhhhhhhhhhhhhhhhhhhhhhh . . .

Vibrating with such intensity that he was on the verge of molecular collapse.

Kshhhhhhhhhhhhhhhhhhhhhhhhhh . . .

Moments away from shattering his sanity like a pane of glass.

Kshhhhhhhhhhhhhhhhhhhhhhhhhh . . .

He shouldn't do this.

Kshhhhhhhhhhhhhhhhhhhhhhhhhh . . .

Couldn't!

Kshhhhhhhhhhhhhhhhhhhhhhhhhh . . .

But that buzzing in his head wouldn't stop.

He just wanted it to stop.

Somewhere amidst the chaos storming against the screen of the television and the bone of his skull in concert, a thought occurred to him.

Kshhhh what shhhh if shshhhhhhh I hhhhhhhhhhhh just hhhhhhhhhhh don't hhhhhhhhhhhh fight it . . .

Frequencies changed.

Wavelengths shifted.

His head flew back in a silent scream. Electronically stunned. For a second the whites of his eyes crackled with static. Every bit of his vision filled with an erratic flicker.

In the glass of a framed picture hanging on the wall, his reflection changed before his very eyes. His face glitched like so many malformed pixels out of sync with each other. Both hot and cold like the shock of arctic water. It surged through his body.

His thoughts, his very makeup no longer his own. Rewriting him.

Rewiring him.

Each limb groaned as they stretched, elongated. Veins became electrical cord woven beneath the thin layer of flesh, breaching the skin—now brittle and blank as cellophane—in some places before dipping back down. Joints and knuckles became servos and gears. No longer soft and pliable, his eyes turned solid as glass while the static raged behind them. A sour, cathode ray chalk burned in his throat and nose, lit by a phosphorous glow against the roof of his mouth. Teeth bared, black negatives of themselves, as it shone like the iron bars of a furnace in front of a blaze. His neck elongated with the same segmented clicks of a stretched antenna. From his forehead two narrow telescopic pieces of thin metal broke the skin and extended outward.

He had been transformed. Violated in the best way. A purposeful way.

Where before he saw only a world he no longer recognized, things suddenly became clear. The static became a voice. From the mouth of a mind that lives between airwaves, born of the collision of so many signals clashing en masse. The endless siege of black and white until all was left dull and gray.

He became the noise.

In that moment the value of human life dropped to zero…and suddenly that crowbar didn't feel so clumsy in his hands. It belonged there.

Evan's face dropped and rose again.

Eyes upcast.

Intent.

His vision, kaleidoscopic and ringed with churning pinwheels. Toxic flowers offered up to him, courting his destructive lust. Skewed forward. Narrowing to points. Strobing. Honing in on what they sought.

Evan, or whoever—whatever—he was now appeared in the doorway. As he wound back with the crowbar and pivoted forward into the room, he let loose a savage yell, crackling with the dirty connection of an industrial speaker.

KSHHHHHHHHHHHHHHHHHHHHHHHHHHHH . .
.

No longer an intrusive onomatopoeia, but a battle cry.

Hank's face froze in shock and terror, a sight never before seen.

He liked it. His lips curled back, showing more of his negative white-black teeth bared in a twisted perversion of a smile.

He swung with the mechanical force of a wrecking ball.

The blow landed hard on the right side of Hank's head, followed by the distinct crack of bone. He immediately dropped to the ground.

For the briefest of moments there was a break in the static.

Surprisingly, there was no blood. Only an elbow-sized depression with an angry purple bruise already swelling beneath the skin.

Hank began to twitch.

Evan rolled him over. A dark stain formed at the front of his pants followed by the smell of urine.

He swung again and the bent claw buried itself in the flesh beneath Hank's chin with the ease of a shovel into snow, poking part of the way out of his mouth, behind the bottom row of teeth. A gurgle issued as blood spilled from the corners of his lips.

With a primal scream Evan yanked upward with the crowbar, taking Hank's jaw with it. A spray of blood and bone in the form of broken teeth went flying toward the ceiling, hit it, and landed back down on Hank's face. Torn skin and cartilage from his larynx was ripped out, and dangling in the nail slot of the crowbar's clawed end, his tongue. Evan lifted the fresh meat to his lips, the organ that made so many words that haunted him, and swallowed it. It was part of him now.

Kshhhhhhhhhhhhhhhhhhhhhhhhhhhhhhhhhhhhhh . . .

"You sssssssssaid...I'd...be back." His voice garbled and spliced with digital interference amidst the ugly hiss of static. Evan choked up on the shaft and slowly raised it above his head. Already he could see the light draining from Hank's eyes.

Kshhhhhhhhhhhhhhhhhhhhhhhhhhhhhhhhhhhhhh . . .

"You werrrrrrrrre...right!"

With one hard downward thrust, he impaled Hank

through the mouth with the chisel end, piercing through the back of his skull with a satisfying final crunch.

He admired him this way. Silent. Blood spilled out across the floor from the wound.

Kshhhhhhhhhhhhhhhhhhhhhhhhhhhhhhhhhhhhhh . . .

The static grew quieter and quieter. Until finally it was gone.

The noise had stopped.

SportsCentre resumed.

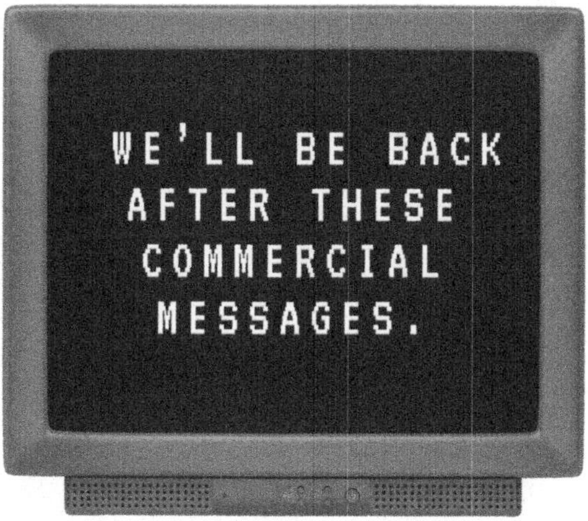
WE'LL BE BACK
AFTER THESE
COMMERCIAL
MESSAGES.

Are You Tired Of Existence?
THE ABYSS
There's nothing like it!
CALL
000-0000

Attention.
Affection.
Acceptance.

Now available 24/7 at the click of a button.
*May cause addiction, obsession, and distorted perceptions for which we are not responsible.

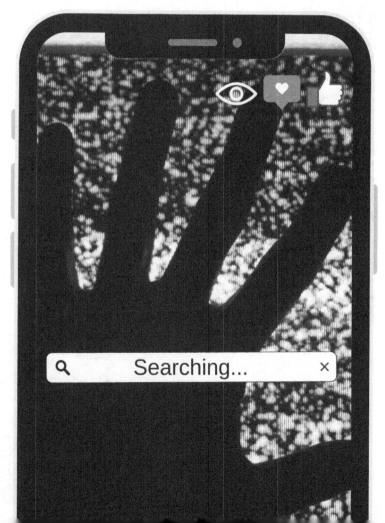

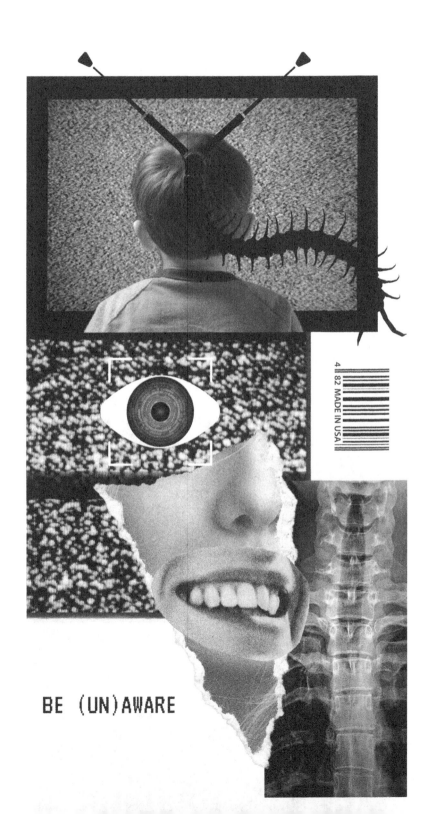

BE (UN)AWARE

One Day (too late)

0 123456 789012

IT'S JUST A NUMBER

IN FRAUD WE TRUST

★ VOTE ★
TODAY!

THINK *outside* THE BOX

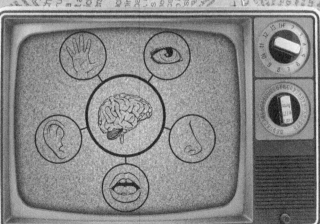

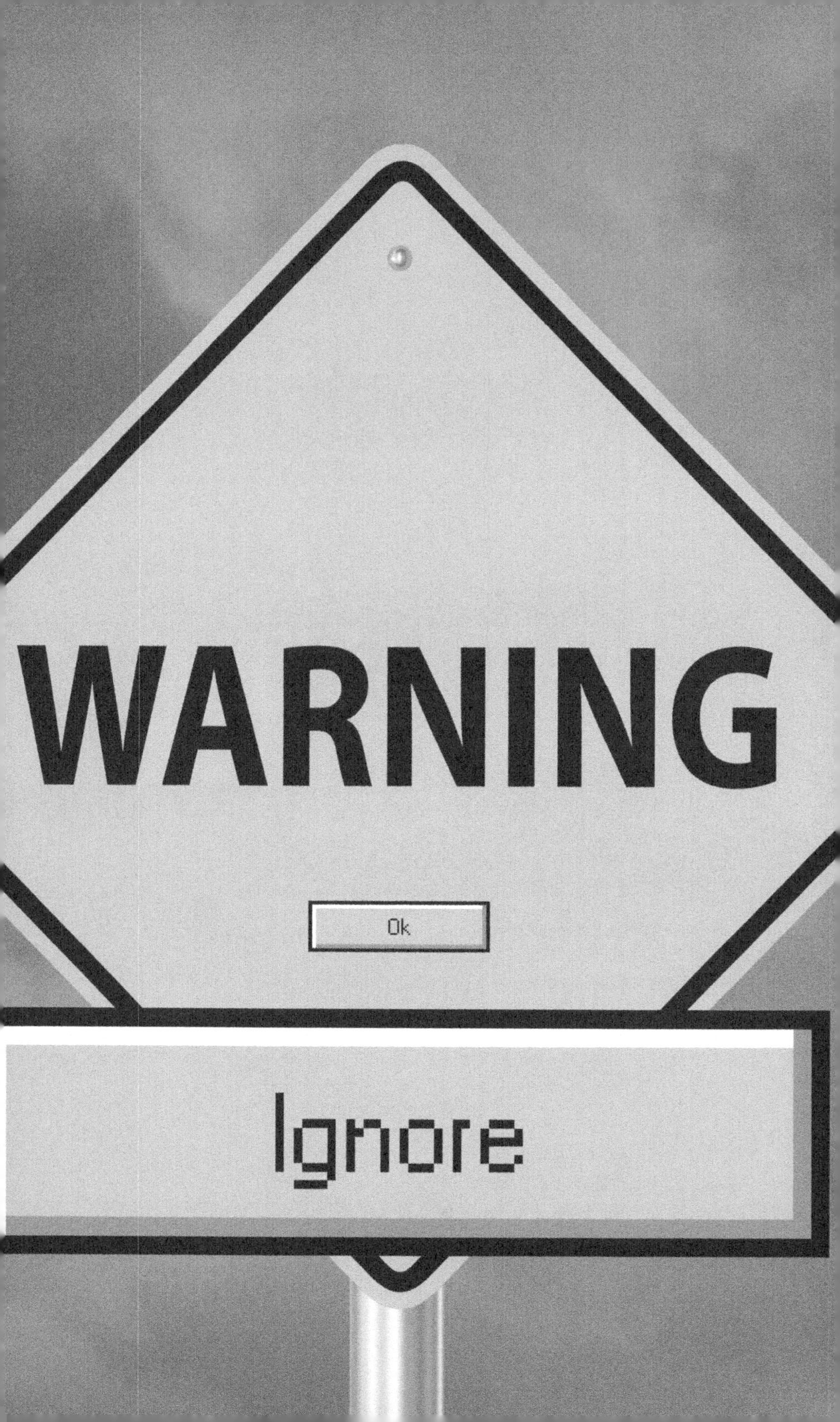
WARNING
Ok
Ignore

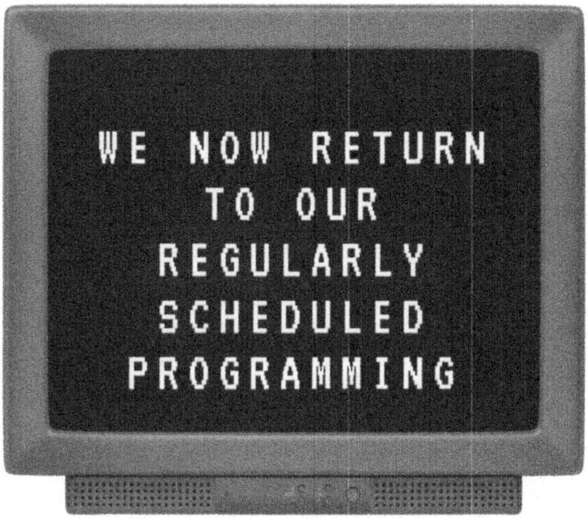
WE NOW RETURN
TO OUR
REGULARLY
SCHEDULED
PROGRAMMING

REVENGE

THE BECOMING

EVAN STOOD THERE, fuming over the body as he slowly returned to his original form.

Looking down at Hank's lifeless, jawless body, in every part of him—machine or man—he couldn't find a shred of remorse.

What he had done was necessary.

A matter of self-preservation.

Whatever it took to relieve himself of the noise.

Noise caused by Hank's macho bullshit. His derision. His discouragement. Evan felt no more sympathy for him than he did a faulty circuit fucking up the picture. Where there had been guilt there was now one frequency. Telling him that this was salvation. And that made this not only right, but righteous.

His fury had been swift and true. A fury begot from a most unexpected of sources. Where he thought the static was there to torment him he now knew otherwise. It was there to test him. It seemed strange without it now. Clearly, the TV had more value than he realized.

Speaking of value . . . Hank has a safe in here.

Evan came around the side of his desk, and sure enough a small metal safe was tucked away into the shadows of the far corner.

Rather than crouch down, he pushed the entire desk back until it was fully visible. A common Sentry Safe, the very model sold right here in the store. This would be a problem for most people, but you don't spend time around a hardware store without picking up a few hacks. All it took to crack it was a Phillips head screwdriver and a coat hanger, both things easy enough to find around the store. Once he snagged the solenoid pin, the bolts slid back and the safe door swung open.

Inside were a few stacks of hundreds, a baggy of a fine white powder, and a gun. A loaded .44 Magnum to be exact. As Clint Eastwood as it gets.

Relief, pure and complete relief washed over him. Here was how he would make those final notices and invoices go away. Here was how he would make the pain go away. Here was how he would visit it upon those who crossed him.

And all he had to do was kill somebody. Somebody no one would miss, except maybe his bookie. Not even his mother. She'd be upset of course upon learning of his fate, but she too would be relieved. He was sure of it.

Eventually.

Evan took it all. Stuffed the money in the cargo pockets of his pants and tucked the gun into the waistband. After diligently wiping any surface he touched clean of fingerprints, he chose to err on the side of caution and check the security footage in the server room. As expected, everything from his arrival until now was nothing but static. He made his way back down the stairs, looking back only to see that the security camera had returned to normal.

The whole drive home he felt...different. Alert. Determined. Deadly. The city itself was different. Where before there was nothing but dark alleys and dirty streets there was now opportunity. Nooks and corners in which to indulge this newfound brand of vengeance. The artificial lights around him as pleasing to his pixelated eyes as the rising sun. He breathed exhaust fumes, replenished by them.

The first thing Evan did when he returned to the store, before disposing of the crowbar, before even changing bloody clothes, was check the TV.

He entered carefully, slowly, as if trying not to alert an intruder in his home. The screen was blank. Showing nothing but the darkened reflection of the store.

Maybe it was just the electricity buzzing from the lights or the drone of traffic from the road, but after having it in his head so immensely, he could still hear it. Even in silence.

He almost missed it.

Evan immediately got to work. First, he popped in a movie. *First Blood.* Seemed only fitting. With the sound of the intro music playing, he ran upstairs and changed clothes. The bloody ones he placed in a plastic garbage bag to dispose of later. The crowbar he wiped clean and kept. It was a part of him now. A friend.

Next he made a sign from the cardboard lid of the empty donut box in thick black marker—BATHROOM FOR CUSTOMERS ONLY. Crude, but it would do until he could have a proper one made.

After that, he texted Brian.

> Hey man. Sorry about earlier. Why don't you swing by tomorrow and let's talk?

For a minute after hitting send, Evan stared at the screen, somehow expecting that a response would come immediately. But knowing Brian, it wouldn't be for a few more hours at least.

"Sorry?" I'm not sorry. Three hours late on his first day, opening *day, and did dick all but be a smartass.*

The noise began to pick up again. Only this time it went with the grain rather than against.

Sure, why don't you swing by later and we'll talk... because that's all it will take to make the noise unbearable again. Then it would be time to meet Mr. Crowbar! (Okay, I'll work on the name.)

Brian didn't have much of anything, certainly no

vault. Although…he did have an issue of Action Comics #23 (first appearance of Lex Luthor). Mint condition if he remembered correctly. That had to be worth something. Or maybe he would stick it in the paper shredder, just because he could. Because fuck it. Why not? Nothing should be precious. Why cling to these tokens of impermanence?

How nice would it be to put out a box of donuts each powdered with strychnine? How good would it feel to pay RETRO VIDEO a visit, see what they were doing differently for future reference, and scorch the place to the ground. He could pay a visit to "Brooke Shields" and take anything she had of value. Every last bit of it.

But why stop there?

Who knew what the extent of this ability was. With the noise to his advantage rather than as a hindrance, he could hit stores. Banks, even. Might the static have some kind of effect on cash machines? Who knew? In time he may be able to slip in and infiltrate anything connected to the internet. Maybe he could already. He could spread this abyssal gospel. Recruit. Many hands make for lighter work, after all. He could start the mother of all doomsday cults that would make Jonestown look like a summer camp.

He could do whatever he wanted. There was no one to stop him.

The possibilities were endless.

He saw forward into his future again. It looked much

different than the forecast from earlier. Collecting different trophies, ones he wouldn't dare display in the store (that could be interesting, though).

Why even stop there? He could topple the corridors of power, like in *Fight Club*.

I am Jack's desire to see everything collapse and burn.

I am Jill's complete lack of originality.

Only not in order to make way for something else. Not to let the Earth recover, rise from the ashes, and see something better form in its place.

To kill what can't be saved.

To turn on the dark for fear of the light.

To erase it all completely.

There were no limits.

He would consume this material world and everything warm in it. Make it cold. Disintegrate it. Every sign and structure that stood, every part of the concrete jungle around him turned to dust. Let the debris pile up until it blocks out the sun. Let every snowcap melt and turn the flooded oceans to a putrid sludge. In time he would find a way to melt the very sky and consume the stars in it. He would watch one final sunrise before seeing that the universe, the entire cosmos, was snuffed of light. Return everything that lived to the bliss of oblivion, all of it lost to a storm of electric fuzz until it was utterly and completely empty.

He was just getting started.

For a second, the TV sputtered with a flicker of static.

Then it was gone.

REMORSE

I DO NOT WANT THIS

EVAN SLUMPED backward against the wall as he slowly returned to his original form. Each breath a welcome relief. And though it had stopped, he could still hear the noise. Hammered and bruised into his brain with its sheer unrelenting force. He had been held hostage to it.

There Hank lay. Dead. Mutilated.

Suddenly he didn't feel so relieved anymore. With the noise gone, the act seemed all the more horrible.

Oh my god, what have I done?

With the crowbar dangling from his hand, resting on his knee, dripping blood, it slipped and hit the floor with a *clang*. Both hands went to his head, rubbing his temples, staring at the severed mandible where it had landed between him and Hank's corpse. Never mind the video store or his mountain of collectibles; this would now be his legacy. This is what he would be remembered for.

As a murderer.

You are now a murderer, little Alex, came the mocking laughter of Mr. Deltoid. *A murderer.*

"No no no no no no," he gibbered to himself. "What have I done?"

You've killed a man...and eaten part of him too, that's what!

Evan turned to his side and spewed the contents of his stomach, a mixture of vomit, blood, and rent flesh onto the floor next to him.

What he had done was necessary. A matter of self-preservation. But no matter how sorry he was, no matter how he regretted it, it was done. And that was it. There was no going back.

He watched as the blood leaking from the back of Hank's head spread closer and closer to him. The full gravity of things now inescapable.

It stopped.

Evan scrambled toward it, dropped, his nose nearly touching the floor to be sure, but it was true. The blood had stopped spreading.

Paused.

Then, right before his eyes, the pool began to recede. So slow at first that he nearly couldn't tell. But sure enough, the thin line of red rolled back and into the wound it came from.

Then the wound healed.

Then the severed mandible leapt off the floor, hitting

the ceiling again and taking the splatter of blood with it as it reattached to Hank's face.

Then he began to twitch in reverse before his eyes were open again and he was back on his feet. His face was one of shock and terror before facing the TV.

Evan's surroundings changed. Every edge of them cut and scrambled by scanlines. Rewound until he went back through the darkened hall outside...down the stairs...past the batwing doors...and back to the parking lot.

He was back in his van where the crowbar reappeared in the passenger's seat without a drop of blood on it. Back to the moment when he thought to himself . . .

If I just hadn't picked up that stupid TV...

Night became day and the parking lot outside Hank's Hardware became his tiny little room above REWIND VIDEO. Next thing he knew, he was sitting up in bed, just as he had been earlier that day.

Evan had seen far too many movies to think it was all just a dream. And if it was, this wasn't a very good movie. Stunned, he picked his phone up from the nightstand.

July 18, 9:27 AM.

Inside his head it was blessedly, and thankfully, finally quiet. Immediately he got out of bed, went to the TV and turned it on.

The static was gone.

He turned it off.

Then back on again just to be sure.

Evan hurried downstairs to check the store. The TV wasn't there. Gone from the middle of the floor where he had left it last night. The slugger and the drill back in their original places. Everything was just how it had been. Which meant that he should be on his way to pick up coffee and donuts.

So that's what he did. He dressed as he had that day. Got in his van and set off on the same route at the same time.

The whole drive there he felt...different. Alive. Humbled. Appreciative. The breeze through the rolled down window felt fresher. The sun felt warmer. The smell of coffee clearer, bringing a smile to his face. The city itself was different. Evan really never minded the sounds of it. The traffic, the honking of horns, the click-ety-clack of trains and subways as they sped along their tracks. There was something to it, especially in the summer. Whatever sights and sounds the day brought, be it the door opening, Huey Lewis and the News, or someone asking to use the bathroom, he would welcome them all with renewed vigor. Because they were better than the alternative.

But . . . he had to see with his own eyes.

He had to know.

Evan made for the corner of Frobisher and Pine. Sure enough, there it was. An old 29" Panasonic vacuum tube television set. Same spot, same sign taped to it. Sitting right where he had found it.

He had been given a second chance.

A rewind.

Were his troubles fixed? No. But whatever he had to face, he sure as hell was not going to make the same mistake twice.

Ever so quietly, Evan thought he heard the static again. Second by second, the volume increased despite no change in the screen.

He knew it wasn't really there, just the echo of it. A subliminal imprint. The suggestion that what had been was seared into his brain as it probably would for a long time to come. Maybe permanently.

But he would survive. He would learn to live with it. In time it may fade as things often do. Gone completely? Only time would tell.

He didn't know that everything was going to work out. There was no guarantee. But he knew one thing—he would try. Hope for the best and do everything he could to make it so. As a statement to himself and to the world that this is how he wanted things to be.

No matter what, he would not let the noise change him. He would not become that thing.

Evan put his foot to the gas and sped away, leaving the TV waiting patiently to see who else might drive by.

Have a nice day.

AFTERTHOUGHT

Since people liked when I did this for the stories in *Acts of Violence*, which is where this one was initially supposed to appear, let me tell you a little bit about where it came from.

The moral is quite simple: don't let the noise in your head get to you. If that's enough explanation for you, thank you very much and you can stop right here.

If not, allow me to elaborate further.

Those who write horror are often asked what they're afraid of. Invariably, they tend to respond with a phobia or a faux wry answer like one star reviews or something like that. Well, here it is. My fears on full display. Why? Because I guess I'm hoping that it will afford me some measure of agency—a facing of the fear, so to speak— and in doing so allow me to rob it of its power.

I'm not afraid of death. I'm afraid of a collapsed ecosystem. I'm afraid of being priced out of life by inflation and cost of living. I'm afraid of seeing everything

I've worked so hard for so long go nowhere or be destroyed due to a misstep. I'm afraid of seeing an idea materialize elsewhere before I can get to it because I'm not working fast enough. I'm afraid of a culture who values influence over substance. I'm afraid of popular opinion prevailing over facts and sense. I'm afraid of an ever lowering common denominator. I'm afraid of cults of thought. I'm afraid of entrenched positions. I'm afraid of what should be an opportunity to communicate with each other being used to silence. I'm afraid of the things I use to cope and give myself some sort of solace and pleasure from these miseries being the very thing that kills me. I'm afraid of ways I've changed long ago still being at risk of returning under the wrong conditions. I'm afraid of feeling like I should remain quiet lest I stir the pot; which can be beneficial in the short term, but in the long term just winds up compromising myself. I'm afraid of not being heard or understood because of the lethal levels of stress and anxiety that come with it. And I'm afraid of that being the takeaway in this one precious life we have to live. So you see, it's not death I'm scared of; it's everything that precedes it.

Despite the beauty and wonder of the planet we live on, the world is a Hell of our own making. For ourselves, for each other, for everyone that has been and everyone who has yet to be. All of that together just makes for one big, constant noise.

All. The. Time.

I wouldn't call myself a cynic, though I have cynical

tendencies. It's not the wolf I want to feed. But some-times you have to. By starving it you just make it meaner. Hungrier. More feral. And that, I believe, is dangerous. Sometimes you have to let that wolf out once in a while. Give it time to roam in order to keep it tame. That's why I write what I write.

I don't know how this book will be received. I'm sure some will probably hate it. It doesn't matter. All I know is that this was one story that just had to come out. I'm not so dewy as to think I'll write about all this and they'll simply go away or bring closure. These things grow back like a stubborn tumor. I'm writing about it because I don't know what else to do. It's what I've got. This was not written to give you or me answers or to make either of us feel good, nor to criticize or fire shots; that is never my intention. I suppose if this book were to have a single label, it would be therapeutic nihilism. Hopefully in sharing it there will be others who think and feel and fear similarly. But then again, maybe not.

I don't want to leave behind a legacy of temporary things. Butchered sheets of paper. Monuments to the ego. I want to inspire people to pick up a pen and start writing. To pick up a brush and start painting. To pick up an instrument and start playing. To say "Yes I can" instead of "It's too late." To say whatever it is they want—whatever they *need*—to say. Even if it's just to give them some comfort and let them know they're not the only ones who think and feel the same things.

This is me with my hat in my hand saying, *Anyone*

else feel this way? Anyone else think these things? Anyone else scared and worried and getting worse? I'm sure the answer to that is yes, but then that makes for yet another question: what do we do about it?

And that's why there are two endings. Whatever the case, I know how I want to approach things.

Do you?

I read Chuck Palahniuk's *Fight Club*, Chandler Morrison's *Dead Inside* and, in case it wasn't obvious from the chapter titles, listened to a steady stream of Nine Inch Nails while writing this book. In doing so, I found that *Dead Inside* mentions *Fight Club* by name and *Fight Club* was "written in stolen moments while listening to The Downward Spiral on park benches." This was not planned by me, just a happy co-incidence, so it seems I was in good company.

I also listened to approximately 40 hours of grey noise. I find it rather soothing.

ACKNOWLEDGMENTS

Thanks to my editor Cara Flannery for cleaning up my mess. To the publisher who flat out told me to send this in during their submission window, but ultimately passed on it (no, I won't tell you which one). To the people who I've dragged into my misery and in doing so may be forcing to relive theirs by reading it early on. As always, to my Tabby for being the best writer's caddy a guy could ask for by reading this when it was just a stick hut of a story, helping me build upward, and for putting up with me and my design changes throughout.

And also as always, thanks to you the reader. Hope you got something out of it.

-MH-

May 26, 2023

ABOUT THE AUTHOR

Marcus Hawke primarily writes horror and dark fiction, some fantasy and sci-fi, and a few things that defy categorization. His works include *The Miracle Sin, Acts of Violence: Twelve Tales of Terror, Bump in the Night,* and a number of anthology appearances. He was born in Toronto and moved around quite a bit during the dreaded formative years before finally settling in Calgary where he studied at the Alberta College of Art and Design. He lives with his feline overlord in an apartment building haunted by the type of neighbors that make a person wish a ghost would come to visit. This is his third book.

Visit www.marcushawke.com for more.

facebook.com/MarcusHawkeAuthor

instagram.com/marcushawke

tiktok.com/@hawke.tok

ALSO BY MARCUS HAWKE

The Miracle Sin

Acts of Violence: Twelve Tales of Terror

Bump in the Night

October Blood (contributor, editor)

Devil's Rejects (contributor)

Anterior Skies, Vol. 1 (contributor)

Forthcoming
The Trouble With Faith and Other Stories

Made in the USA
Coppell, TX
15 August 2023